MOMMY'S BEST KISSES

For Owen
—M. A.

For Ben and Lulu, with kisses times ten
—S. W.

Mommy's Best Kisses
Text copyright © 2003 by Margaret Anastas
Illustrations copyright © 2003 by Susan Winter
Manufactured in China. All rights reserved. No part
of this book may be used or reproduced in any manner
whatsoever without written permission except in the
case of brief quotations embodied in critical articles and
reviews. For information address HarperCollins
Children's Books, a division of HarperCollins
Publishers, 1350 Avenue of the Americas, New York,
NY 10019.
www.harperchildrens.com

Library of Congress Cataloging-in-Publication Data
Anastas, Margaret.
    Mommy's best kisses / by Margaret Anastas ;
illustrated by Susan Winter.— 1st ed.
        p.   cm.
    Summary: Animal mommies lovingly kiss their
animal babies.
    ISBN-10: 0-06-623601-0 (trade bdg.)
    ISBN-13: 978-0-06-623601-8 (trade bdg.)
    ISBN-10: 0-06-623606-1 (lib. bdg.)
    ISBN-13: 978-0-06-623606-3 (lib. bdg.)
    ISBN-10: 0-06-443839-2 (pbk.)
    ISBN-13: 978-0-06-443839-1 (pbk.)
    [1. Kissing—Fiction. 2. Parent and child—Fiction.
3. Animals—Fiction. 4. Stories in rhyme.] I. Winter,
Susan, ill. II. Title.
PZ8.3.A525 Mo 2003
[E]—dc21   2002014412
Typography by Stephanie Bart-Horvath
❖

MOMMY'S BEST KISSES

by Margaret Anastas

illustrated by Susan Winter

HarperCollinsPublishers

I kiss your small hands
as you reach for my face,

I kiss your sweet neck—
it's my favorite place.

I kiss your five fingers
that squeeze mine so tight,

I kiss your strong arms
and you squeal with delight.

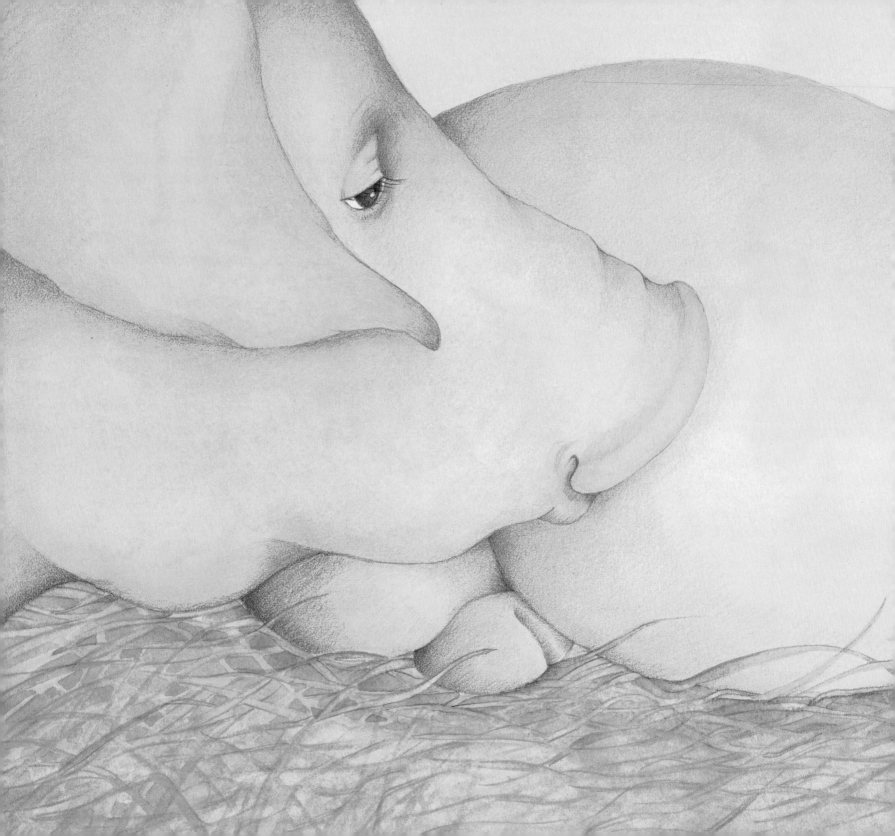

I kiss your plump tummy
as round as can be,

I kiss your belly button
as you grin up at me.

I kiss your pink knees
while you laugh and you wiggle,

I kiss your ten toes
and you let out a giggle!

I kiss your wee nose
as you smile playfully,

I kiss your rosy cheeks
and you gurgle with glee.

I kiss the soft hair
on your sleepy head,

I kiss your drowsy eyes
as I put you to bed.

I kiss your dear face
and I whisper good night,

I blow one last kiss
while I turn out the light.

So tonight when you sleep
dream of kisses times ten,

And tomorrow we'll start
all over again!